This book belongs to

....

Walt Disney's

Pinocchio

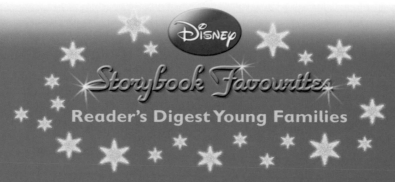

Disney

Storybook Favourites

Reader's Digest Young Families

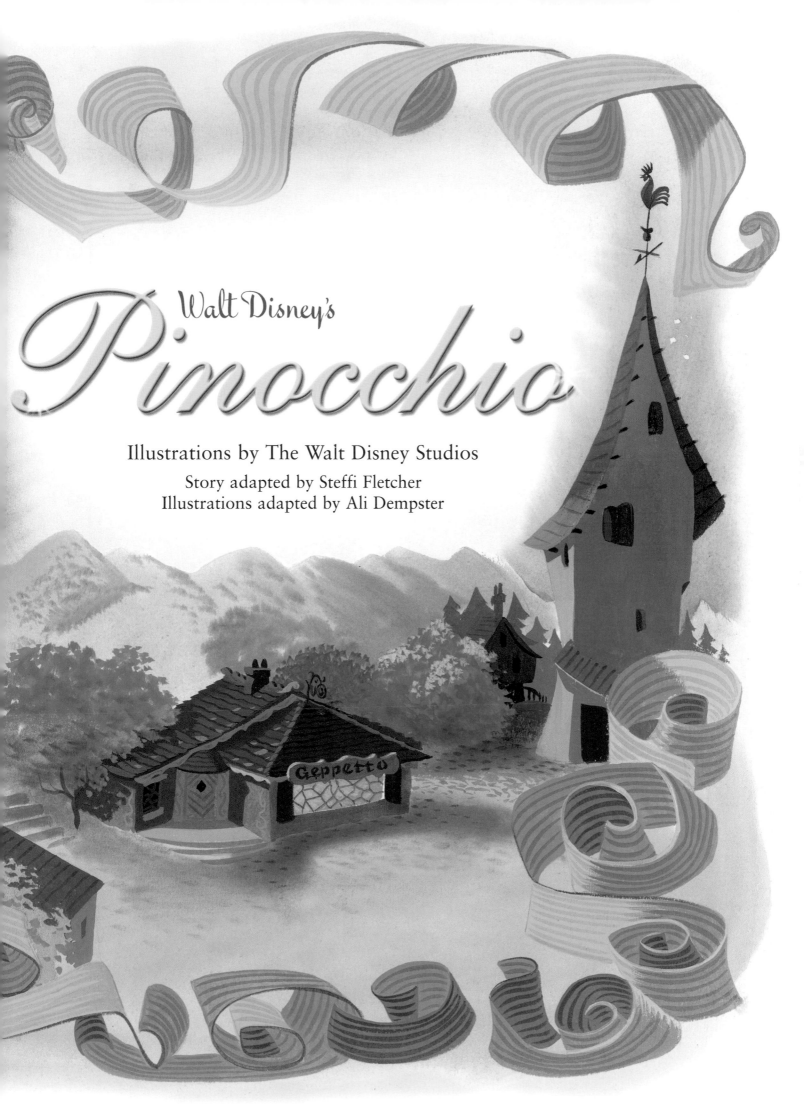

Walt Disney's

Pinocchio

Illustrations by The Walt Disney Studios

Story adapted by Steffi Fletcher

Illustrations adapted by Ali Dempster

One night, long, long ago, the Wishing Star shone down across the dark sky. Its beams formed a shimmering pathway to a tiny village, whose little homes lay deep in sleep. Only one house still had a light burning in the window, and that was the workshop of Geppetto, the kindly old wood-carver.

Geppetto had stayed up late to finish the merry-faced little puppet he was carving. Now he held up the puppet. 'Look, Figaro! Look, Cleo!' he said with a chuckle. 'Isn't Pinocchio almost like a real boy?'

The only answer was a snore. Figaro had his soft kitten nose folded into his paws, and Cleo lay sleeping in her goldfish bowl.

'Sleepyheads!' The old wood-carver sighed. Climbing into bed, he mumbled, 'I wish you were a real boy, Pinocchio!'

Somebody overheard Geppetto's wish, and that was Jiminy Cricket. All evening Jiminy had sat hidden behind the hearth. He had seen how kind and gentle the wood-carver was, and he felt sorry for him because he knew the lonely old man's wish could never come true.

Suddenly, a shimmering light filled the room. Jiminy gasped. Out of the light stepped a beautiful lady dressed in shining blue. She raised her wand and said, 'Wake up, Pinocchio! Skip and run! Good Geppetto needs a son!'

Pinocchio blinked his eyes and raised his wooden arms.

'I can move!' he cried. 'Am I a real boy?'

'No,' the Blue Fairy said sadly. 'Prove yourself brave, truthful and unselfish, and some day you will be a real boy.'

'But how can I do that?' asked Pinocchio.

'You'll have a conscience to help you!' Looking around, the Blue Fairy beckoned to Jiminy to come out of his hiding place. '*Sir* Jiminy Cricket,' she said, 'I dub you Lord High Keeper of Right and Wrong!'

'Now, remember, Pinocchio – be a good boy and always let your conscience be your guide.'

The next morning, Geppetto couldn't stop rubbing his eyes. For there before him was the puppet he had carved the night before, laughing, chattering and running around the workshop!

'No, no, it can't be true!' said Geppetto. 'It's a dream!'

But Pinocchio ran to him and threw his wooden arms around his neck. 'It's true, Father!' he cried. 'It's true! I'm alive!'

Then Geppetto realised that a miracle had happened and he was overjoyed. He looked proudly at Pinocchio. 'But now, Pinocchio, you must go to school,' he said. He brought out a pile of schoolbooks. 'Study hard! Then you'll become a real boy!'

Pinocchio nodded happily. 'Goodbye, Father!' he shouted, and off he marched, his books under his arm, full of good intentions.

Meanwhile, Jiminy Cricket had overslept and now jumped up in a great hurry. Quickly, he stuffed his shirt into his trousers and rushed out. 'Hey, Pinoke!' he called. 'Wait for me!'

Panting, he caught up with Pinocchio just as the little puppet was walking off arm in arm with the worst pair of scoundrels in the whole countryside! The villains were a fox called J. Worthington Foulfellow and a silly cat called Gideon.

'Yes,' the sly fox was saying to Pinocchio, 'you're too talented a boy to waste your time in school – isn't he, Gideon?'

Gideon nodded.

'With that face, you should be an actor, my boy!' said Foulfellow.

Pinocchio thought that was a wonderful idea.

'But, Pinoke!' cried Jiminy. 'What will your father say?'

Pinocchio looked startled when he saw Jiminy. He said angrily, 'Oh, Father will be proud of me!'

Jiminy knew Pinocchio was being silly. But he had to stay with him because the Blue Fairy had made him responsible for Pinocchio's conscience – helping him to know right from wrong.

Soon they came to a puppet theatre. When Stromboli, its owner, saw Pinocchio, his small evil eyes lit up. 'What a lucky card!' he cried with delight. 'A puppet without strings!'

The fox nodded. 'And he's yours,' he said, smiling greedily and holding out his paw, 'for a certain price, of course!'

That night, Pinocchio sang and danced on stage with the spotlight on him, just as Foulfellow the fox had promised. The audience clapped and cheered and roared for more. A puppet without strings! It was a miracle!

Jiminy, sitting in the audience, felt terrible. You'd better congratulate Pinocchio and go off ... alone, he thought sadly to himself. What does a great actor need a conscience for?

After the show, Pinocchio held out his hand to Stromboli and said shyly, 'Goodbye, sir, and thank you. Shall I come back tomorrow?'

Stromboli smiled an ugly smile. 'Not so fast, young man,' he snarled. 'You're mine, and you stay here!' And *bang*! – before Pinocchio could resist, he was locked inside a birdcage!

When Jiminy came backstage, he was very shocked to find Pinocchio shut up in a cage!

'Oh, Jiminy,' Pinocchio sobbed, 'why didn't I go to school? I'll never see my father again!'

Jiminy tried to pick the lock, but without success. Gloomily, he sat down next to Pinocchio, not even noticing how the room began to glow and grow brighter. Suddenly, the Blue Fairy stood before them!

'I'll help you this time,' she said, 'because you are truly sorry. But run home now, Pinocchio, and be a good son, or you'll never become a real boy!'

And as she waved her wand, Jiminy and Pinocchio found themselves standing on the open road again!

'Phew!' Pinocchio sighed thankfully. 'Let's go home, Jiminy!'

The two friends started running as fast as they could, when whom should they bump into but Foulfellow and Gideon!

'Pinocchio!' Foulfellow cried. 'My dearest young friend! How does it feel to be a great actor?'

'Awful!' said Pinocchio. 'Stromboli put me in a cage!' And he told Foulfellow how badly he had been treated.

The sly fox pretended to be deeply shocked. And before Jiminy knew what was happening, Foulfellow had persuaded the puppet to forget all his good intentions about going home and take a restful trip with him to Pleasure Island.

'Pinocchio!' Jiminy cried. 'You promised to go straight home!'

'I will, later on! But now, I need a rest after my terrible experience!' Pinocchio said.

They came to a coach that was going to Pleasure Island. It was pulled by small donkeys and filled with rude, noisy boys.

As Pinocchio climbed aboard, Jiminy saw the sly Coachman slip Foulfellow a heavy bag. Again, the fox had sold Pinocchio!

The Coachman cracked his whip, the boys shouted, and the coach started. The only ones who didn't seem happy were Jiminy and the small donkeys.

After boarding a ferry, the coach and its passengers soon docked at Pleasure Island. The boys piled down the gangplank and into the streets. Here there were bands playing, streets paved with cookies and lined with doughnut trees, and fountains spouting lemonade. The Coachman kept urging the boys, 'Have a good time – while you can!'

And they did! They climbed the ice cream mountains and sailed down the lemonade river. They smashed windows, burned schoolbooks and teased the poor little donkeys. Pinocchio made friends with the very worst of the boys, a mischievous bully named Lampwick.

Some days later, down on Tobacco Lane, Jiminy found
Pinocchio puffing on a corncob pipe. Lampwick had a big cigar.
Jiminy lost his temper and shouted, 'This has gone far enough!
Throw away that pipe and come home this minute!'

Pinocchio looked sheepish, but Lampwick began to snigger.
'Don't tell me you're scared of an *insect*!' he laughed nastily.

'Gosh, no, Lampwick. That's only Jiminy. He can't tell me
what to do!' And Pinocchio blew a puff of smoke right into
Jiminy's face!

Jiminy was about to march off angrily when suddenly Lampwick grabbed his head, and Pinocchio cried, 'Jiminy, my ears are buzzing!'

Jiminy was shocked. Before his eyes, the boys were sprouting donkey ears! And Pinocchio had grown a tail, too!

'It's donkey fever!' whispered Jiminy, horrified. 'You were lazy, good-for-nothing boys, so now you're turning into donkeys. Let's get out of here!' They dashed through the streets, which were strangely deserted.

As they went round a corner, they came face-to-face with the Coachman. He and armed guards were rounding up a bunch of braying, howling donkeys, many of which still wore boys' hats and shoes.

'There they go! Those are the two that are missing!' shouted the Coachman. 'After them!'

Pinocchio and Jiminy rushed towards the wall surrounding the island. They managed to scramble up, but when they looked down, they saw a little donkey dressed in Lampwick's clothes. It *was* Lampwick.

'Go on, Pinocchio!' Lampwick cried. 'It's all over for me!'

There was nothing they could do. Sadly, Pinocchio followed Jiminy and dived into the sea.

They had a long, hard swim to the mainland, and a longer, harder journey home. It was now winter in the village, and through the drifting snow they hurried to Geppetto's door and pounded on it.

The only answer they heard was the howling of the wintry wind. Pinocchio peered into the window. The house was empty!

'My father's gone away!' said Pinocchio, and a tear ran down his long nose and froze into a tiny, sparkling icicle.

Just then, a gust of wind blew a piece of paper around the corner. 'Hey, Pinoke!' Jiminy exclaimed. 'It's a letter!'

The little cricket began to read the note aloud:

'Dear Pinocchio,

I heard you had gone to Pleasure Island, so Figaro, Cleo and I started off in a small boat to find you. Just as we came in sight of the island, out of the sea rose Monstro, the giant whale. He opened his jaws and in we went. Now, dear son, we are living in the belly of the whale. But there is very little to eat here, and we cannot exist much longer, so I fear you will never again see me.

Your loving father,
Geppetto'

For a while, both Jiminy and Pinocchio were silent, too upset to speak. Then, in a determined voice that Jiminy had not heard him use before, Pinocchio said, 'I'm going to save my father!'

'But Pinocchio,' cried Jiminy, 'think how far it is to the ocean!'

'I don't mind,' Pinocchio said firmly. 'I must find Father.'

Just then a soft voice said, 'I will take you.' And out of the sky fluttered a small white dove with a golden crown on its head.

Pinocchio stared. 'You?' he asked. 'How could *you* carry us?'

'Like this!' said the dove as she began to grow and grow. 'Climb on,' she ordered them, and off they went. All day and all night they flew, until they reached the high cliffs of the seashore.

They landed. 'Goodbye!' called the dove. 'Good luck!' And she flew away. What Pinocchio and Jiminy did not know was that she was their very own Blue Fairy in disguise, and that it was she who had brought them Geppetto's letter.

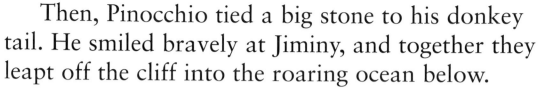

Then, Pinocchio tied a big stone to his donkey tail. He smiled bravely at Jiminy, and together they leapt off the cliff into the roaring ocean below.

Down, down, down they went, through the green water, past clumps of waving seaweed. At the sandy bottom, Pinocchio scrambled to his feet. 'Come on,' he said. 'Let's find Monstro the Whale.' He started off, peering into every grotto and green sea cave.

'We'll never find him,' muttered Jiminy.

But Jiminy was wrong. Very near them floated the whale they were looking for, fast asleep. Inside the whale, at the far end of its mouth's dark cavern, Geppetto had built a strange house, made from bits of ships that the whale had swallowed. He had also made a fishing rod to catch the fish that swam into the whale's mouth. But Monstro was sleeping, so no fish came in.

'Not a bite for days, Figaro,' Geppetto said sadly. 'If Monstro doesn't wake up soon, we'll all starve.'

Geppetto sighed and went on fishing. Figaro was so hungry he began to sneak greedily towards Cleo's fishbowl.

Geppetto saw him. 'Shoo!' he shouted. 'Shame on you!'

Just then, Geppetto felt a nibble. 'Food at last, Figaro!' he cried. But when he landed his catch, it wasn't fish at all. All he'd caught was a book called *101 Ways to Cook Fish*.

As Geppetto turned the pages, his mouth was watering. Slowly his eyes were drawn to Cleo. Moving as if he were in a nightmare, Geppetto started to scoop the goldfish out of her bowl. But as he was about to drop her in the frying pan, he realised that he could never really eat his little pet.

'Dear Cleo,' he begged, 'please forgive me!'

It was a solemn moment. They all felt that the end was near.

And then the whale moved!

Monstro gave an upward lunge, and through his jaws rushed a wall of black water. And with it came a whole school of tuna!

Swimming in the sea nearby, Pinocchio saw all the fish fleeing. He caught a glimpse of Monstro coming towards him. Then he, too, was sucked down through those huge jaws.

Close by, Jiminy bobbed up and down in a bottle, begging Monstro to swallow him, too. But the whale went back to sleep.

Deep inside Monstro's mouth, Geppetto was catching fish after fish. 'Food!' he yelled. 'Oh, Figaro, Cleo – we are saved!'

He was so busy, he scarcely heard a shrill cry of 'Father!'

'Pinocchio?' he asked wonderingly, and turned around. 'Oh, my own dear son!' he exclaimed. 'Is it really you?'

With tears in his eyes, the old man embraced Pinocchio. But when he lovingly took off his son's hat, out popped the dreadful donkey ears.

Pinocchio turned his face away in shame. 'I've got a tail, too,' he admitted sadly. 'Oh, Father!'

'Never mind, son,' Geppetto said gently. 'The main thing is that we are all together again.'

'And that we escape from here,' Pinocchio added.

'We never will. I've tried everything … I even built a raft …'

'That's it!' cried Pinocchio. 'When Monstro opens his mouth, we'll float out on that raft.'

'But, no,' argued Geppetto. 'When Monstro opens his mouth, everything comes in – nothing goes out.'

'Yes,' said Pinocchio thinking, 'it all comes in if he swallows. But not … not if he sneezes! Quick, Father, help me build a fire!'

Before Geppetto knew what he was doing, Pinocchio gathered up a pile of chairs and crates and set fire to them.

As the fire began to smoke, they got the raft ready. The whale grunted. Suddenly, he drew in his breath and gave a monstrous *SNEEZE*! Out went the raft into the open sea!

But they were still not free. The angry whale saw them and plunged after them. With one blow he shattered their frail raft.

Geppetto felt himself sinking. 'My son, you must save yourself!' he cried.

But the brave puppet swam to him and kept him afloat. Giant waves swept them towards dark rocks looming against the shore. Just as they were about to be crushed against the rocks, they were washed through a tiny crevice into a lagoon. In vain, Monstro hurled his weight against the rocks, trying to reach them. His prey had escaped!

Geppetto lay on the beach, filled with gratitude to his son. Then he saw Pinocchio lying beside him – still, cold, and pale!

A fishbowl floated up to the water's surface. A bedraggled kitten clung to the edge of the bowl, and beside it bobbed Jiminy Cricket, still in the bottle.

But neither Cleo, Figaro, nor Jiminy could comfort the heartbroken old man as he wept bitterly, feeling sure that his wooden boy was dead.

The old man gathered poor Pinocchio into his arms and went home. When he reached his cottage, he sank down and prayed.

Suddenly, a ray of starlight pierced the gloom. A soft voice said, as it had said once before, 'And someday, when you have proved yourself brave, truthful and unselfish, you will become a real boy …'.

Pinocchio stirred and sat up. He looked at himself and felt his arms and legs. Then he knew!

'Father!' he cried joyfully. 'Father! Look at me!'

The Blue Fairy's promise had come true! Pinocchio was no longer a puppet! Pinocchio was a real, live, flesh-and-blood boy!

Walt Disney's Pinocchio is a *Disney Storybook Favourites* book

Walt Disney's Pinocchio, copyright © 1953, 2001, 2004 Disney Enterprises, Inc.
Story adapted by Steffi Fletcher. Illustrations adapted by Al Dempster.

This edition was adapted and published in 2009 by
The Reader's Digest Association Limited
11 Westferry Circus, Canary Wharf, London E14 4HE

Editor: Rachel Warren Chadd
Designer: Louise Turpin
Design consultant: Simon Webb

® Reader's Digest, the Pegasus logo and Reader's Digest Young Families
are registered trademarks of
The Reader's Digest Association, Inc.

We are committed both to the quality of our products
and the service we provide to our customers.
We value your comments, so please do contact us on
08705 113366 or via our website at
www.readersdigest.co.uk
If you have any comments or suggestions
about the content of our books, email us at
gbeditorial@readersdigest.co.uk

Printed in China

A Disney Enterprises/Reader's Digest Young Families Book

ISBN 978 0 276 44455 5
Book code 641-014 UP0000-1
Oracle code 504400001H.00.24